# DEAD BEATS

## CASE SOLVED

*This book is dedicated to
my family who always
believed in me*

# Foreword

When I first began writing *Dead Beats: Case Solved*, I didn't expect it to become such a whirlwind of adventure, twists, and imagination. What started as a simple idea—three friends receiving a mysterious note—soon spiralled into a complex tale of secrets, technology, and bravery. The characters of DJ, Kate, and Sam quickly took on lives of their own, each adding humour, heart, and heroism to the journey.

This story is more than a mystery—it's about trusting your instincts, standing by your friends, and pushing forward even when things seem impossible. I wanted young readers to feel the thrill of cracking clues and chasing down danger, all while experiencing the warmth of friendship and the power of clever thinking.

To those reading this: thank you for stepping into this world with me. Whether you're here for the mystery, the magic, or the memories, I hope you enjoy every page. And remember—sometimes the biggest answers come from the smallest clues.

# Preface

In a quiet town filled with secrets and silence, three curious boys stumble upon a cryptic note that sets off a chain of mysterious events. What starts as a summer break filled with camping plans and arcade visits soon turns into an unforgettable mission to solve a dark puzzle threatening their neighbourhood.

*Dead Beats: Case Solved* is a thrilling tale of friendship, courage, and clever thinking. It follows DJ, Kate, and Sam as they piece together strange clues, battle digital traps, outsmart villains, and ultimately bring justice to their town. Inspired by my love for solving puzzles and telling stories, this book is my way of saying: *every mystery has a clue—you just have to look closely.*

I hope you enjoy the adventure as much as I enjoyed creating it.

*— Jishnu Dornala*

# CHAPTERS


1. The First Note

2. The Creepy House

3. Virtual Reality

4. Vacation Gone Wrong

5. Clues

6. Suspicion

7. Mr. Grimm

# Chapter 1
# The First Note

It was the last day of school. DJ was excited for the holidays. He skipped that day as he was too excited to plan a trip to the woods.

 His best friends Kate and Sam also skipped school to hang out with DJ. They wanted to help but also wanted a good excuse for skipping school. They scoured the internet to find rental cars, camping spots, tents, etc. His laptop was starting to glitch as it was an old one.

 By the time it resets, the boys thought of heading downstairs to check any mail. There was a lot of junk mail but one of those piqued their interests. It looked fancy and shady. They opened it and it read:

*Darkness is my home. Catch me if you can. 7th house to your right.*

*1 2 5 2 5*

They became suspicious and wanted to go to the 7th house to their right, but DJ was thinking about what the numbers meant. Suddenly a thought struck him.

He said to them, " What if it is the date of a random day?" They decoded it to 12th May 2025. That was the next day. They planned on going to that house the next day.

It was lunch time and the three of them had lunch in DJ's home. They were served lentil soup and vegetable wrap. While eating they watched their favourite channel on the television. It was their favourite magician "Mr. Magic"
This time the setting was in an arcade. He made tickets appear out of his hat and made them disappear. He had many tricks up his sleeve.

DJ noticed a card in the background. He knew that most of the magicians used green or blue screen for their background but not Mr. Magic. It was placed on a simulator game just before it entered the ticket slot. It had the same handwriting. He said the same to Kate and Sam and also suggested to go to the arcade the next weekend. They were eagerly waiting because it was their first time going. DJ was more concerned about the card.

Lunch was over and they went upstairs. The laptop was back to normal, and they continued to surf the internet. They found a good tent that could fit five to six people. It also had a net that would prevent mosquitos from entering the tent. Next, they were thinking about the campsite. They saw the perfect one that was owned by VG. He tried to search "VG" up, but it didn't show any results.

They liked that campsite a lot, so they selected it. Next was a rental car. They needed a good one that could fit five or more people. They looked up on SUV's and also MPV's. They liked a luxurious MPV which was a "Viper". They liked its features and automatic transmission and also its boot-space. They selected it. It was a little expensive, but it came with its benefits.

It was evening time, and the boys went out to play football. DJ was exceptional in speed, agility and dribbling. He was the best striker out there. Kate was a mid-fielder who gave the best assists and was also very good in pin-point passes. Sam was a defender. He was someone who gave strikers a nightmare. He was very good in guarding and stealing the ball.

They played a quick match with their other friends. DJ dribbled past the mid-fielder, faked a defender and scored a banger against the goalie. Kate gave a beautiful, curved pass to DJ who simply acted like he was about to touch the ball, but he didn't. The goalie was faked into going to the left side, but the ball found the top corner and it was a goal. The play started with a counterattack from the opponent's team and the striker kicked the ball with all his power, but it was easily defended by Sam. Sam cleared the ball towards the goal and to his surprise it went in. The score was 3-0.

The match ended and everyone went to their homes. DJ returned to his home ate some spaghetti and went to sleep.

# Chapter 2
# The Creepy House

The next day, DJ woke up, brushed his teeth, had a bath and ate his breakfast as fast as possible. He went to the 7th house to his right and found that Kate and Sam were already there.

He asked if they had their breakfast. Kate said, "A couple of waffles" and Sam said, "PB&J".

They slowly went inside. It was a haunted house. They were searching for a light switch as it was very dark. There was a small window with its curtains shut closed. Sam went and opened the curtain. The house brightened up a little.

They found a doll. It was not scary, but it had blood droplets. They were creeped out, but they were also curious. They slowly touched the doll, and a secret tunnel opened with doors.

They randomly picked a door and to their surprise it was just another dark room. After they entered the tunnel Kate heard some weird sounds. He continued to walk without telling anyone. Now everyone started listening to louder sounds. They were investigating every corner and nook, but nothing was out of the ordinary other than the sounds. They saw a wall with a threatening message that read "I'm going to get you". They didn't know what to do.

They were led to some stairs by following arrows that were written on the wall. Each floor had the floor number. When they went to the 2nd floor, they saw the shadow of something. After they went to the 3rd floor, they saw a man dressed up as a pilot. He came closer and closer.

They ran inside a room and locked it. It was a bedroom. The man started to break the wooden door with his axe. The boys didn't know what to do. The door slowly started to break. They saw a window. Sam took out the bedspread and tied it to the leg of the bed. Kate and Sam climbed out safely. They asked DJ to come fast. Just then the door opened. DJ took a wooden chair and hit the man with it. He blocked it and was about to swing his axe. DJ rushed to the window and jumped out. They heard even more noises.

Kate said, "Don't they sound like kids?" DJ and Sam were able to corelate.

The three of them were terrified. When DJ went home, he saw his dad starting the bike. He asked his dad what the matter was. His dad informed him that Suresh, their house servant, was being beaten up by Mahesh and his goons. He also told DJ that Suresh's land was illegally occupied by Mahesh.

Mahesh demanded money. If the money was not paid by the next day, he threatened that Suresh's house would be demolished. DJ's dad being a kind man he was went to Suresh's village and paid to Mahesh.

Mahesh left. DJ's dad took Suresh to the hospital. After 2 days he was cured. Suresh thanked DJ's dad.

Suresh didn't even take his salary for the next 2 months.

DJ turned on the television to get distracted. He wanted to see Mr. Magic but saw Light Square instead. The scrolling screen read, "Andrew lived in a community with his family and friends. He was 9 years old. One day while he was playing, he was bit by a termite and got so much pain. He couldn't sleep because of the pain. The next day he discovered some strange things occurring in his body. He was able to run on the walls without any help. He was able to run 200 mph. When he was attending school, the teacher asked the question. He gave the answer as 2, he then turned his wrist and became invisible. Everyone in his school was shocked. He did it again and was visible.

 Day by day he discovered different things, and he knew that he had become a superhero. He ran so much that he was 70 trillion times faster than the speed of light. One day he discovered a feature and noticed that he was the god of lightning. He stopped crime every time.

He built himself a suit. It contains a mask, a sweater, and a pair of sweatpants. It was amazing. He once battled with a foe who was very stubborn. He just used tricks to defeat him." DJ lost interest. He thought Light Square was good as Sam highly recommended it, but this was just average. He thought of going to the arcade with Kate and Sam

# Chapter 3
# Virtual Reality

The three of them went to the mall. They entered a lift and clicked on the 5$^{th}$ floor button. The lift was packed with people. They searched for the arcade but only found the food court. They went to the 4$^{th}$ floor and checked. There it was. They entered the arcade and bought a play-card that cost a fortune.

They hesitantly bought it and went to the VR section. There they recognized the adventure game, and Sam started playing it as he was the best at VR games.

After about what felt like an hour the tickets started rolling out and so did the card. DJ and Kate asked how the game was and asked Sam to explain what took so long. Sam started telling his virtual adventure, "I was merrily walking along the road with two other fellas.  I think their names were Steve and Jack. After We reached their home, I had a warm glass of milk, and we started eating breakfast. Then Steve wondered and asked us that

they were having waffle for breakfast in that pleasant summer, what the nicholes will eat. Jack said that the nicholes won't eat during early summer. Then we got an idea. We went on a Jetpack to the cloud sector.

On our way we encountered a mysterious black hole. We thought of avoiding it, but it gobbled us up and teleported us to planet TCF-21. We had to get out of there, but we were trapped in a dungeon! The weirder thing was that it had advanced technology. To get out of there I had to make a blast. I took nuclear objects and some TNT.

The cage opened with a blast. We ran till what seemed like an exit, but it was a trick. The exit was way back. We avoided the lasers as much as we could and got out of there. I was drenched in sweat. We went to the cloud sector and greeted the Saint Nicholai and nicholes.

The nicholes and Saint Nicholai refused to take the juicy fresh fruits that were offered with kindness. Well, it was worth a shot I thought to myself then. While coming back we were again teleported to the lair of the dragon. To get out of the place we had to defeat the surgeon zombies and the dragon of almighty.

The twist was if the surgeon zombies touched us, we would travel back in time and again travel forward in time and again respawn. So, we thought of avoiding the surgeon zombies by either dodging or fighting back. We first tried to dodge. One cheeky zombie touched me, and I respawned. I knew that I had to fight back, and I did the same. I punched one on the face and kicked one on the neck. After a lot of moves and action, the surgeon zombies were defeated.

The dragon of almighty was the only thing left so; we launched a three-assault on it. I smashed the dragon's teeth of its gum. Jack cut the tail of the dragon. Steve punched the dragon's stomach. At last, we kicked the dragon with all our power and the dragon of almighty was defeated. That's what took so long. The dragon was having a Kevlar armour, don't ask me why. The X button was also jammed." DJ and Kate loved the story and wanted to play it themselves. DJ stepped in and put on the VR headset. He had a severe headache after putting it on. Then after another hour he came back to his senses. Kate and Sam had to manually remove the VR headset. Sam said that the chip was hacked by a local user and the hacker trapped DJ in it. DJ asked why Sam didn't get affected by that.

Sam said, "I think it is because I activated a firewall in the game. You played the same game, right? Then how did you get hacked?"

DJ said that he didn't play the same game. Sam asked what game he had played. DJ explained the game, "I was welcomed into the castle by some woman. Lucky for me she was good and kind. She took Me to Sir Madveric (The God of dragons). I was guided my way to a court room which was made a mess by the people. A guy named Lucas came towards me and clapped at my face! Horrified I stepped aback. The people were laughing and mocking at me. It seemed that Lucas was a bully or a prankster. The main person, whose name was Xinochi, entered the class to talk about how to use a dragon twig. He was talking about the spells. "Almazanto! means summon the dragons," said the master, who was sippin' his drink. Then he gave a book, which was only having one page, to everyone. It seemed that all the spells were written in that '*One-page* book'.

The master then took us to the dragon home. It was where all the dragons were kept. "Oh, I almost forgot to tell my name. My name is DJ sir," I said, waving my hand to the master. "Weird name," said the master, in a low and loud voice. When we went outside, I thought we were learning about how to check the horizon, but the master had proven me completely wrong. We were learning about how to ride a dragon. I was riding with master Xinochi himself! He instructed me to hold the dragon near the neck region but gently.

Almazanto - summon the dragons

Laxunophinto - cast the glow strike

Traxino - Back off

Lujeffo - Be banished to the sun

Lujetro - Be banished to the water

Luphinito - Be banished to the glow strike

Lujeffito - Be banished to the trielements

I thought to myself that if I screw this up, I might just lose all my impression in front of the master. I want to be the daring but good kid. Twenty-five other I held the dragon there. Now he told me to hold the rope and steer. But I didn't know how to steer.

So, master held my hand and made me do it. After a while, I was flying the dragon myself. I was imagining what could be more relaxing than riding a dragon above an ancient castle in the past. It was a ride of a lifetime.

Every kid landed safely into the terrain spot. I went to something that looked like a canteen.

Thinking and eating, I suddenly choked something that looked like pasta. A second later it was Lucas who came to my place to apologise for what had happened.

I was unsure if I had to accept the apology or just ignore him. I chose neither of the options and stayed quiet. It was night-time and everyone went to either second or third floor of the castle to sleep. I think I saw a big glitch in the game when I was riding the dragon. I suddenly fell off but came back in." Sam thought for a while and said, "Maybe that glitch was the point of time the hacker hacked into the game. Did you hear anything weird in the game?" DJ said, " The same thing that was written in the first junk mail we saw."

Kate said, "We need to find out who this guy is."

DJ said, "Did you hear the news about the children who mysteriously disappeared? They were last seen near a post-box that was near the 7th house. Maybe the same man hacked into the arcade game. His house was dark, and you know what the note said right. Anyways, I need to pack for tomorrow."

DJ went to his home and started packing.

# Chapter 4
# Vacation Gone Wrong

Next day DJ's family were going to a tourist spot. Their family rented Viper car for the tour. DJ and his father left DJ's sister, mother, and grandmother at the top and they went back home for a cap and a grill. DJ slipped near the veranda and fell. Lucky for him he landed safe and sound. He quickly went upstairs and got the cap and returned downstairs. He looked for the grill almost everywhere but couldn't find it. He looked in the kitchen, the living room, the storage etc. "Well, the grill is not there," DJ said with disappointment. They thought of returning to the tourist spot after DJ had chocolate chip pancakes.

DJ and his father opened the boot to check if the tent was there and to their surprise, the grill was right beside the tent. They hopped on the car with excitement and zest.

They were listening to some songs before they finally reached the ghat road start point. After 20-30 minutes the roads were so high that most of the vehicles struggled to move.

DJ's car went a bit high but suddenly the engine turned off and the car started to fall. It rolled back and landed safely. The car wouldn't start. DJ's father said, "Someone placed a rope in the middle which made the car suddenly roll." DJ agreed. As the car rolled backward, a thick cloud of dust rose around it, filling the air and blurring everything in sight. They asked many people for the direction to the nearest police station. One guy who was drinking coconut water told them that the nearest police station was 500 meters away.

They entered the police station which looked very old from outside. But when they went inside, it was so modern. They went to the S.I (Sub

Inspector) and explained everything that had happened.

The S.I was ready to take up the case. She investigated the area and noted down some points. They went into the forest area to check for clues. All they found were dried leaves and sticks placed oddly on the ground. Suddenly they heard a growl. They looked around to check what it was. It was a wild boar. It was ready to attack with its full power. "Quick, climb the tree," the S.I screamed. DJ and his father agreed. Two seconds later they were all sitting on the hard branches of

the tree. "We can't stay like this until that thing goes," DJ's father said.

DJ took a torch from his pocket and pointed at the boar's eye. With pain the boar ran away screaming. "That torch is really bright," the S.I said. After they got down from the tree, DJ saw something that looked like a remote. It had six buttons with each one labelled.

He pressed a button, and the trees split open and shook the ropes placed on the road. Luckily, no

19

one were crossing that part of the road at that time.

He showed it to the S.I and she kept the remote in a zip lock cover for evidence. After looking around for some time, they found a cave. They went inside it to find some bad guys who were controlling the ropes with the remotes. "Alex! You left the remote on the floor after you came back from the first spot," a bad guy shouted. "Time to put in the bars," DJ said with a smile. "Oh yeah? You and who," another guy asked. The S.I walked in and said, "How about me?" The bad guys were terrified and started running but the police had them surrounded. The bad guys went to jail.

"Your kid has good presence of mind," the S.I told DJ's father. "What can I say. He is just a very smart kid," DJ's father said to the S.I.

DJ and his father then headed towards their car and drove to the tourist spot. Over there, they setup the grill and spent the rest of the day setting up the tent. The next day they packed everything and were ready to leave. After everyone sat on the car, DJ kept the radio. "Kids are being kidnapped. Parents are advised to not send their kids to play," the man on the radio said. DJ knew it all along. The information was delayed.

# Chapter 5
## Clues

The ride to home was silent. No one in the car wanted to talk after hearing a thing like that. DJ didn't sleep that day. He was thinking about the kids who were kidnapped.

The next day, he called Kate and Sam over to his house to solve the case. The three of them searched for clues in town but couldn't find any.

One day as they went downtown, they saw a new shop named 'Kidnap: Saloon and Spa'. They thought it was a little weird to name a shop like that, so they went in. The building was not ready yet. The three friends were on the ground floor. They couldn't find any clue. With rage, Kate stamped on the carpet. There was some metal sound. The friends removed the carpet, and they found a basement door.

They opened it and saw some stairs leading
down. They went down the stairs to investigate.
There was nothing but an old restaurant. No one
were there so they thought of going back up. But
they saw a register. In that the receptionist only
wrote one name.

The friends thought it was quite odd that someone
knew this place. So, they went through it.
Suddenly a man came out from the restroom and
started walking towards the main desk.

The friends had to hide. They hid under the desk,
hoping that the man wouldn't see them. "The man
might be the receptionist," DJ told Kate and Sam.
DJ told a plan to Kate and Sam. After that DJ left
the hiding spot and acted as if he just came to the
restaurant.

The receptionist sat on the chair and felt heavy
breathing near his legs. He was about to check
below the desk but, suddenly DJ came towards
the receptionist and said, "My father comes to this
restaurant right," in a British accent. "Yes sir," the
receptionist told DJ, thinking to himself that he
was the son of 'Vlad' the only person who came to
the restaurant. "My father told me that he has
some work, and he went yesterday but didn't
return home. He always told me that he comes to
this restaurant so, I came here for his
whereabouts," DJ told the receptionist. Kate and
Sam were talking to themselves, and Kate said,

"DJ's acting skills are so good." Sam agreed. The receptionist told DJ that Vlad went to the town security camera room.

He also told DJ that Vlad had something planned for that night. DJ thanked the receptionist and asked, "Mind if you drop me home. My father always says that it's not safe to go alone in the night." The receptionist agreed and both went to the ground floor after the receptionist locked the door.

Kate and Sam stole the spare keys and unlocked the Basement door. "It won't go," Kate whispered to Sam. "Here, let me try," Sam said after taking the keys from Kate. But it didn't work. Sam pushed the key and finally to their relief, the door opened.

They went straight to their homes after locking the door. Just after Kate and Sam left, the receptionist arrived and went inside.

# Chapter 6
## Suspicion

The next day DJ brushed his teethed and had a bath so fast that the breakfast wasn't ready yet. He took permission from his father and went to Sam's home. Kate was already at Sam's home, and they were waiting for DJ.

The three of them went to Sam's room and started remembering what had happened the day before and they were searching for clues. Just then Sam turned on his T.V. In the news channel 'Down-Town', the reporter said that another kid was kidnapped at 12:00 midnight in Orangeville.

 "It all makes sense. Vlad is the guy we are searching for. Yesterday he must have gone to the town security camera room, so that he can study the places that don't have a camera near them and kidnap the kids nearby. But he needs permission to enter the security camera room. So, he must have someone in the police force who helped him," DJ said to Kate and Sam. "Quick, to the town security camera room," Sam said. They arrived there after twelve minutes of bicycle-riding. To convince the security guards to show the CCTV recordings, Sam said that someone stole his money. The security guards asked, "When was the money stolen?" Sam replied that it was stolen the day before when he was going to buy medicines for his grandmother.

The security guard said, "You do know that kids should not go at night. You must have seen in the news and radio. Then why did you go at night?" Sam said that his grandma was suffering from extreme stomach pain. The security guard was finally convinced, and he showed the CCTV to Sam and Kate. Meanwhile, DJ went to a security guard who acted suspicious. That security guard knew that DJ was known for his intelligence.

So, when DJ mentioned the point of the kidnaps that were taking place the security guard cried, "I don't know anything about Vlad. Please leave me. I am innocent." "BINGO," DJ exclaimed. "Guys we have found our corrupt security guard. It's Mr. Adam himself." "How did you know that," Adam the security guard asked. "Well, it was kinda easy.

Firstly, I was only talking about the kidnaps as a responsible citizen of our town, and you were worrying so much. Secondly, I had a doubt on Vlad, but I didn't even mention about him to you and even if you did know, the media will cover it and broadcast it to the news, but no new channel of our town has broadcasted that message."

Everyone in the room were shocked. DJ called the police and Adam was arrested. Then DJ started thinking about where Vlad might be. Then something hit his mind. He thought to himself,

"Why was Vlad the only man who came to that restaurant? What was the wooden thing at the end of the room. If Vlad had to get to the place where he would keep the kids, he needed to lock the basement door first and then go from there, but spare keys are not given to anyone as per the instructions given inside the restaurant. Then he must have used the wooden door at the end of restaurant." Kate and Sam were thinking the same thing.

 "Quick to the restaurant" the three friends said at once. They first thought of going to DJ's house to calm down. In DJ's house Kate and Sam were also eating breakfast with DJ. After they were done, they washed their hands. DJ said to his father, "Dad, no more kids will be kidnapped from today. I need to go out for around one and a half hour."

DJ's father accepted his permission. The three friends went to the restaurant. Kate had brought the basement key and opened it. They went inside after locking the door. They went till the end of the room. They saw a wooden door. They opened it and there was a tunnel pathway.

The three friends crawled their way for 30 mins until the tunnel suddenly expanded. They saw another door and they opened it with a lot of effort.

# Chapter 7
# Mr. Grimm?

DJ said that it was Mr. Grimm's house. Mr. Grimm was using the bathroom when the three friends entered his home. The three of them heard muffled screams coming from the basement. They saw another tunnel. DJ asked Kate to go through the tunnel and see what was on the other side. Kate went and was shocked. It was the 7$^{th}$ house. He heard a little girl cry. He went there and quickly grabbed the girl and came back through the tunnel.

They quickly went to the basement and opened it. The kidnapped kids were there! The three friends were shocked. They opened the cloth that covered the children's mouth and untied their hands that were tied with ropes. A second later they heard loud footsteps coming towards the basement. Kate told DJ what he had seen

The kids were so scared. DJ, Kate, and Sam couldn't understand why. Mr. Grimm came down the basement and saw us. "You pesky friends. How did you find the kidnapped kids," Mr. Grimm asked with a low voice.

"It all makes sense. Your full name is Vlad Grimm. No wonder your house is connected to the restaurant in the basement downtown and no wonder you are a dear friend to Adam." Sam said.

"You are the kidnapper" DJ shouted out loud. "You kidnapped the kids who lived in houses that didn't have any cameras near them. Wait a minute. You are in a very bad financial state. Everybody knows that. You have a tunnel that leads to the haunted house. You asked that man to kidnap all the kids and send them to your house via the tunnel. I saw that every kid was last seen near the same post-box. You and that man will share the money you get from their parents and most of it goes to you.", DJ added.


"You went to Bruce's house? No wonder you are smart, but now it is useless because you are going to be locked in here forever," Vlad said and laughed maniacally. DJ laughed and said, "Well, not if I called the police just the second, I reached your house." The police had Vlad surrounded and he was sent to prison, and the kids happily went to their homes. DJ, Kate, and Sam were awarded with detective badges.

In the prison, Vlad asked DJ to come near him, and he whispered to DJ, "I will be back kid!" DJ laughed and said, "You want to go to prison more than one time? Well, that's fine with me."

After 10 days, summer holidays were over, and the new academic year had started.  DJ told Kate and Sam, "I hope this year we will learn about firewalls. I don't want to get stuck in virtual reality again." The three of them laughed.

# THE END…